Smiley's DreamBook

a BONE tale by Jeff Smith

COLOR BY TOM GAADT

An Imprint of Scholastic Inc.

All rights reserved. Published by Graphix, an imprint of Scholastic Inc.,
Publishers since 1920. SCHOLASTIC, GRAPHIX, and associated logos are
trademarks and/or registered trademarks of Scholastic Inc.

The publisher does not have any control over and does not assume any
responsibility for author or third-party websites or their content.

Library of Congress Control Number: 2017939969
ISBN 978-0-545-67477-5
10 9 8 7 6 5 4 3 2 1   18 19 20 21 22

Printed in China   38
First edition, August 2018
Book design by Jeff Smith and Steve Ponzo